W9-BBD-730

THE SECRET JOURNEY OF THE SILVER REINDEER

# THE SECRET JOURNEY OF THE SILVER REINDEER

LEE KINGMAN

ILLUSTRATED BY LYND WARD

DOUBLEDAY & COMPANY, INC.
GARDEN CITY, NEW YORK

Library of Congress Catalog Card Number 68-12736

Printed in the United States of America
First Edition

*To Lisa and Betty Nätti*

NORTH OF THE ARCTIC CIRCLE as it swings across the European continent is a region known as Lapland. Early history called it Thule or Ultima Thule, and later, Finnmark. The Lapps, who call themselves the *Samer*, began their nomadic journeys in this area long before the boundaries of the countries as we know them today—Norway, Sweden, Finland, and Russia—were established. The borders of these countries, which were so often at war with each other, changed many times during the centuries, but the Lapps continually crossed and recrossed them as they followed the seasonal migrations of the reindeer. Now that Norway, Sweden, Finland, and Russia are independent countries with fixed borders, the Lapps have had to conform to the regulations of grazing and registering herds set up by each country—and nowadays they are more apt to be called Norwegian Lapps, Swedish Lapps, Finnish Lapps, and Russians.

The Lapps are, however, a race apart—unrelated in origin or language to other peoples. Their nomadic life and general isolation has contributed to slight regional differences in their clothing—most obvious in their dramatic hats—and in their vocabulary. Under modern conditions this isolation is disappearing, for the amphibian plane can land anywhere in the lake-strewn, bog-filled tundra country. Lapp children are now sent to boarding schools, where they learn about their history, modern reindeer management, and the Lapp language is taught before it, too, is lost.

The Lapps are tough people, hard-working, practical, and persistent. As a race they are small-statured and seldom look heroic. But they have survived centuries of difficult nomadic life under some of the harshest conditions in the world. Also in the period of World War II, when Finland fought two short but costly wars in rapid succession with Russia and Germany, the Germans in their retreat through Finnish and Norwegian Lapland devastated the countryside. People, herds, herd dogs, houses, whole villages were destroyed. Invaluable artifacts and much of the few written records of Lapp history which existed were lost.

Today the surviving Lapps are adjusting to a world where their whole traditional life is changing. But their life and deeds in the past have always contained elements of heroism as they have struggled against the overwhelming odds of nature and fate. Their early religion saw gods and spirits in many kinds of inanimate objects and their own tales are full of magic and mystery.

It is in a spirit of admiration for a wild beautiful country so wide to the horizons that it casts its own spell; for its staunch inhabitants and the magic and mystery interwoven with the hardship of their lives, that the story of Aslak, as it might have happened some years ago has been imagined and written down.

*Lee Kingman*

Blood Ledge
Gloucester
April 1967

THE SECRET JOURNEY OF THE SILVER REINDEER

IT WAS IN THE FAR NORTH COUNTRY of Lapland, where the winter days are brightened only by starlight and glistening snow and the summer nights are dimmed only by heavy clouds crossing the sun, that young Aslak undertook a secret journey to save his family and his herd of silver reindeer.

It happened in the days when the Lapps, or Samer as they call themselves, could still migrate with their herds through Lapland far above the Arctic Circle; and this story began with Jouni Magga. He was a small but sturdy man, whose fight with a giant brown bear, whose luck with nuggets of gold, whose pride in his silver reindeer made him a legend. For who had sat by the hearth of his tent and talked of great hunters and herdsmen and not talked of Jouni Magga?

"He was the greatest of herdsmen," some said, for his deer shone like a silver river in moonlight and ran as fast as the silver streak of the lightning.

"He was a giant among hunters," some said, for only a man of great courage could have killed the biggest bear in all Lapland.

"He was a wizard!" some said, for they thought only a wizard skilled with a magic drum could have found such gold.

Now Jouni Magga fathered three sons. The oldest, also named Jouni, was thrown from a sledge when a lad and half-smothered in snow. So he grew strong in body, but dim in mind. Gentle and kind, he did as he was told. Everyone called him Small Jouni.

The second son, Piera, was wild and reckless, fond of racing deer and making wagers, of fighting and scheming. After he lost two herds of his own through betting and a part of Great Jouni's herd through folly, his father reluctantly said, "You must leave my household and make your own way in the world, for I will give you no more. You may claim nothing from me as long as I live, even though I love you with all my heart and send you away in sorrow."

The third son, Tuure, was a faithful herdsman and skilled trail finder, who took joy and pride in the hard life of a nomad. As long as Great Jouni lived Tuure obeyed his father's orders.

When Great Jouni died, Tuure became head of the family. He cared for his mother, his brother Small Jouni, his wife, and

his five children, of whom Aslak was the oldest. He was proud of the famous herd of silver reindeer which then numbered three thousand animals.

But though Tuure was a man of skill and courage, he had none of the luck of Great Jouni. A winter of the worst ice and sleet in a century cut down his herd by half, and the spring which followed threw brooks into treacherous torrents which drowned hundreds of the winter-weakened deer—and his wife. On the late autumn trek, a miserable journey of cold mists and sudden blizzards, Tuure fell ill of a mysterious disease. Neither the skill nor the herbs of Old Grandmother could save him. In the midst of their difficulties, fifty of the best beasts strayed or were stolen. While other Lapps came to the winter village looking forward to friends and the fun of the fair, the widow and grandchildren of the Great Jouni Magga arrived in sorrow and in fear.

"Someone has cast an evil spell over us and our herd," mourned Grandmother. "And who is left nowadays who has

skill with the drum to tell me how the spell can be broken—and who has cast it?"

"Who believes in the drum?" asked Aslak, even though he had heard much of his grandfather's skill with it. "The church has told us there was never magic in the drum anyway."

So Aslak went to the mayor of the village, to report that fifty of his beasts were missing and he felt they were stolen.

The boy's tale upset the mayor. "Aside from murder, the theft of deer is the most serious charge you could bring. We have had no deer thieves in Lapland for years! You know each herd owner has his mark cut in the ears of his deer and that mark is respected." But as he saw the worry in Aslak's deep black eyes, he could not scold him further. "No, think on it, boy. Your journey was plagued by mists and storms. Your father was raving with illness, tied in his sledge. Your uncle Small Jouni knows summer from winter and a deer from a dog, but that is all. And strong as you are, you are not practiced in herding your deer through a hazardous journey. The deer were lost—not stolen. But the most serious matter, now that your father is dead, is what will become of you and your brothers and sisters?"

"That is no problem," declared Aslak. "I shall take care of my brothers and sisters and Old Grandmother and Small Jouni. It is no one's concern but my own."

The mayor smiled, but he shook his head. "You are only fourteen. And how old are the others?"

"By the time of the spring journey I shall be fifteen," Aslak said grandly. "My sister Merja is thirteen. My brother Pirkka is twelve. My sister Terhi is ten. And my little brother Petri is three. And don't forget Old Grandmother is always full of advice. Among us we know how to lasso and break deer, how to slaughter and skin them, how to make sledges and clothes, how to milk deer and make cheese. We know all we need to know to keep our herd together and let it increase."

Again the mayor smiled and shook his head. "Five children, a weak old woman and a dim-witted man could never survive the yearly journey of the deer. I have talked with the pastor and the teacher, and I have gone over the laws. The pastor and I believe the herd can be sold so that Old Grandmother may be taken care of and you children may stay at school together. We will have no trouble finding buyers for your deer."

"I do not wish to sell. Nor does my grandmother."

"Then I shall speak to her."

"No—I will talk with her," Aslak decided. "It is my duty to take care of her. But she would not be happy without us and the deer. So I must do what is best."

"You must do as your elders tell you, young Aslak," said the

mayor severely, "whether you feel it is best or not."

But to that Aslak could not agree, and he parted from the man in silence, now bearing a burden of disapproval as well as anxiety.

Because he had promised, on his return Aslak asked Old Grandmother, "Are you too weary to make the journey with us this year? Would it ease you to stay at the village and rest while we see to the herd?"

And Old Grandmother had looked at him as if he were a little and ignorant child. "How could I rest, knowing you needed me?"

"It is true," said Aslak soberly. "And it is much to ask. But I do need you."

"Not more than I need you and I need the only way of life I know," she told him. "But you must be my strength."

"I will," promised Aslak. And bravely he told the mayor, "We will not sell our deer."

"We shall see," the wise man replied. "By the time of the spring journey, you may change your mind."

IT WAS A WINTER to break a man's heart as well as a boy's. Again ice sheeted the snow, and the deer struggled to reach the moss far beneath. With their heads deep in the drifts, they were helpless victims of stealthy lynx and wily wolverine. Watch must be kept day and night, so Aslak and Merja took turns with Small Jouni and sharp-eyed Pirkka.

And throughout the long, dark, cruel winter the mayor's doubt gnawed at Aslak. Was he really man enough to keep his family and his herd together? Did the mayor and the elders have no reason for faith in him? Or was their real concern not the survival of five children, a simple man, and an old woman—but the fate of the silver-coated reindeer? Was someone scheming to take the herd away from him?

Grandmother grew weaker and wondered aloud if she would live to see the sun shine once more. One night she woke Aslak.

"I have had a dream," Grandmother said, "and you must

take me on a journey at once. I must go to the camp of Kuisma, the witch-wizard, for I dreamed that he will help you keep your herd when I am gone. I know someone is scheming against you and plans to take your herd away."

Aslak was frightened to hear her confirming his own worries. Was it the mayor—making good his threat to talk good sense into Old Grandmother about selling the herd? Or was it the pastor, exhorting one of his fellow parishioners vigorously about the sternness of God and urging her to stay within reach of the church? Or was it the teacher, convincing her that her grandchildren should be safe and educated in school?

So Aslak was curious about Grandmother's dream. While he didn't really believe in wizards and drums, he could not spurn any way of keeping the herd and his family together.

He wrapped Grandmother in furs and tucked her into a sledge, tying it behind Fleet One, a buck broken to sledge-pulling but swift enough for racing. He put on his skis, and they raced through the forest, surprising deer and beasts of prey alike until they came to a frozen lake.

The old woman told him which stars to sight and on what far shore of the great lake he would find the tent of the wizard. The bitter wind froze silver tears on his cheeks, but Aslak did not falter. Nor did Fleet One. In three rushing hours, silent except for the howl of distant wolves, they reached the *kåta* of the wizard, and Grandmother called out her need of him.

Up through the smoke-hole of the *kåta* flew a snowy owl who stared in silence at the night visitors. The deerskin door flap parted to allow a pure white dog to come outside and glare

at them. Then the owl hooted once and the dog barked twice and from inside came the words, "Enter, you who seek the wisdom of the wizard."

Aslak took Grandmother in his arms and carried her in. But he waited until the wizard pointed to a place on the reindeer skins by the hearth before he set her down. Then the wizard threw a handful of twigs to brighten the fire while he seemed to study their faces. Aslak saw the oldest man with the youngest eyes. His hair was white, as silver as ice, but his smile was as kind as summer.

"You are troubled, old friend," he said to the woman. "Tell me what knowledge you seek."

"Sorrow and woe and misfortune have been the lot of my son and now my grandson. It is beyond bad luck and bad weather, for others have not suffered in these years as have we. Tell me, O Wizard, what evil spell has been cast over the family of the Great Jouni Magga? Who has cast it? And how can the spell be broken?"

The wizard took up his magic drum, and Aslak watched in fascination. When the church had warned against the drums, many were burned and destroyed. But here one was, with symbols for reindeer and mountains and rivers and bears and gods and storms and floods and fire and herbs and health and evil and death etched on its taut old skin. As the wizard tossed the toe bone of a deer on the drum and began tapping, he closed his eyes.

With a start Aslak recognized the wizard. Of course! He was really blind Kuisma, who wandered to the winter fairs and about the summer camps, singing old verses or making up a *joik* —fresh words about new events sung to a familiar tune. He was a minstrel who brought news and knew everything.

Or was he a scoundrel, pretending to be blind and letting people feed him and care for him? Could he see his way under downcast lids? Is that how he could roam unerringly from camp to camp? Once out of sight he probably strode wide-eyed and farseeing! Aslak stirred uncomfortably. Had he just made a three-hour journey to see a wizard who was no more than a pretender?

Then Kuisma opened his eyes and seemed to look right through Aslak. "I see before me a boy who does not believe in the magic of the drum because he does not believe in me. He thinks because he sees me wide-eyed by my hearth I am not blind. But let him learn that the brightest eye can be unseeing, for it is the spirit that sees all."

He closed his eyes again and tapped the drum, while the toe-bone danced across the symbols. Aslak watched in wonder as the bone stopped by the reindeer and then skipped to the mountains and circled the symbol for evil, while the wizard, without looking down once at the dance of the bone on the drum chanted, "Reindeer you seek were parted from you on the journey and led to a different winter ground, and beware, O beware, the man who returns them to you."

Aslak felt a strange chill of fear, for although he had faith in his own knowledge and strength, who does not fear the unknown? Could he succeed in saving his family and his deer against forces beyond his control? Was he unwise to try?

While Aslak made himself stop trembling, the wizard ceased his chant, but swayed in rhythm to his tapping. The owl silently dropped to his shoulder and the dog suddenly appeared at his side. The only sounds were the whip of the wind around the *kåta*, the snap of the twigs on the fire, and the "Tip-tip-tap, tuppy-tup, tap, tip, tup" of the drum. Aslak felt the wizard was not there inside himself at all! And he saw that Grandmother, too, was nodding and swaying, her eyes dark and unseeing.

For a long time it was thus, while Aslak found he could not reason out his fears or his beliefs. It was as if he tried to keep his mind shut against some power that pried and pulled to reach inside him. Then the wizard's fingers suddenly whirred across the drum. The owl hooted. The dog barked. The wizard moved and stirred the fire, and Grandmother held out her hands to its warmth.

Kuisma turned his bright-blind eyes to Aslak. "Listen well, for when you reach your home tonight there will be only you alive to tell the tale."

A terrible tremor of fright shook Aslak, but Kuisma kept on, as if haste were now important. "There is a man who wishes harm to you because you have the goods and wealth of the Great Jouni Magga. It is his second son, your Uncle Piera, who hearing from afar of his father's death, returns to claim an

inheritance. He has upon him some sign he says will prove Great Jouni left all to him. So it falls upon you, Aslak—son of Tuure, grandson of Great Jouni—to disprove him. You must find the true sign for yourself, so you may keep your grandfather's gold of the river Karasjoki, and the silver-coated reindeer. And with them, care for your younger brothers and sisters. You must stand firm but run fast. You must visit old places but seek new trails. You must reach the Cave of the Great Hunters in the Mountain of the Eagle's Head before your enemy. And now already time is rushing past you like the wind. You must return and rescue your brothers and sisters before it is too late."

"Grandmother, stay here with the wizard," Aslak begged, unwilling to take her to her death. "Let me send a band of strong men to bring you back tomorrow."

"I care not about tomorrow," said Grandmother. "Only that you, who are the image of Great Jouni himself, shall break the spell put upon you by my deluded son Piera. You have courage. You must use it."

By the dimming firelight, the owl and the dog and the wizard slept, and on the magic drum the toe bone of the deer rested on the symbol of the mountains. Aslak carried his grandmother to the sledge, and they fled across the frozen lake and into the forest.

WHEN HE REACHED his *kåta*, Aslak picked up his grandmother and, carrying her in, quickly unwrapped the furs about her. To his joy she was still alive. The wizard was wrong!

Then Aslak saw that by the hearth sat the mayor and beside him a man he did not know.

Grandmother stared piercingly at the stranger. Then she said, "I could not go until I knew for certain that my heart no longer yearned for a lost son, and I tell you now that I believe the man who has returned is no true son to me. Aslak, remember this night and all you have heard. Now let me depart."

She lay back, and very soon she died, as surely as if she had been wrapped in skins and pushed away in a sledge to die alone in the snow, which once was done with the old in this cold land.

Merja and Terhi, huddled on the women's side of the hearth, began to weep. "Oh, how sad that Grandmother could not really see well enough to know her own son after all these years. Aslak, the man by the hearth is Uncle Piera, and he has brought back the fifty reindeer lost upon the trail this autumn."

Piera Magga smiled at Aslak. "When I heard all the sad things that befell my father's family, I hurried to help and on my way it happened that I found fifty silver reindeer with the Magga mark. So I brought them to join the herd. I mourn that my mother's mind was too worn to know me, as were her eyes. But now that I am here, I will be head of the family and responsible for you all."

"Uncle Piera has brought us handsome knives!" exclaimed Pirkka. "One for you and one for me."

"And beautiful needle cases to hang on our belts!" exclaimed Merja. "One for Terhi and one for me."

But in Aslak the strange forecasts and the cold terrors of the night formed into resolve, and he found strength even in the death of his grandmother.

"Give back the knives and the needle cases," he ordered, "for we cannot take gifts from him. I am the head of the family. Did you not hear my grandmother reject this man just now? Besides I have been told Great Jouni sent him away saying he could claim no more."

"Ah—" said Uncle Piera, "let me point out that my father did not mean to disinherit me on his death. No! He said only that I could claim nothing from him while he lived. Nor have I!

I have suffered many misfortunes since I was sent away without asking for one reindeer. Is that not true? Have I ever claimed so much as a discarded antler from my father's deer? Have I not now returned fifty straying reindeer to the herd?"

Aslak acknowledged that his uncle had made no claim.

"But I have spoken with the mayor and wise elders of the parish council, and they tell me you are too young to bear responsibility for a herd and a household. So the responsibility is mine as your uncle. And something more. You know of the famous nugget—the Luck of the Karasjoki?"

"Indeed," said Aslak, for he had heard many times the tale of how his grandfather's good fortune began.

"Everyone knows Great Jouni Magga's good fortune began the day he found that large nugget on a bank of the Karasjoki. Or rather, what he found were *two halves which fitted together so perfectly not a reindeer hair could slip between.* He showed this to us often when we were boys, and he always said that whoever possessed the Luck of the Karasjoki should possess the herd—because then he would have the luck and the skill to take care of it. And now—look—"

Uncle Piera reached into the pocket of his embroidered *atsas-lieppa,* the dickey which filled the neck of his tunic. Unrolling a cloth, he held out a rough object which gleamed dully in the firelight. "Here it is—half of the Karasjoki nugget, sent as a sign for me to return and become the head of the family."

But Aslak stared at it, keeping his face as blank as the snow. "How did you come by this? Can you prove that this is half of the true Karasjoki nugget that belonged to my grandfather?

Do you know where the other half is which matches it?"

"Two years ago at the winter fair at Kautokeino I met Kuisma, the blind peddler. When he heard I was Piera Magga, he cried out, 'Like the wind I have been searching the length and breadth of the north country for you. Your father is dying and he entreated me to find you and give you this talisman saying tell my son here is half of my luck—a sign that he must return and make the luck of the Magga whole again.' As to where the matching half is, surely that would be among Great Jouni's possessions—the box of secret belongings which every man of wealth collects during this lifetime, and which must have been kept by my mother after his death. By rights it is here in this *kåta* and I demand that you give it to me."

Aslak sat still, feeling again the trembling chill that shook him in the wizard's tent. But he knew he must be strong and test his uncle to find the truth.

While Merja and Terhi watched, their faces drawn with dismay, Aslak took off his four-peaked cap. Loosening the drawstring inside, he poked into one of the tips and held out what looked like a dirty rock. "Let us see if between us we have the whole then of my grandfather's nugget, for it is I who have the other half."

He heard his sisters stir with excitement, and Pirkka moved restlessly toward him.

Aslak explained. "When my father, Tuure Magga, could no longer speak, he pressed this into my hand. Until I looked, I thought perhaps he had followed the old way of choosing a rock or a stick with a face to be his good-luck god. Since so much ill-fortune followed us, I was tempted to throw it away.

But when I looked, I found it half a nugget of gold. Now—hold out your half and see if yours is the mate of mine. For if it is, then my grandfather must have decided to divide the luck and the herd between you and my father—that is, if your message be his true words. If it is not, then I believe you have come to deceive us."

The boy and the man reached toward each other in the flickering light of the fire. The mayor edged closer to observe most carefully. Merja sucked in her breath and Terhi wiggled impatiently. Aslak knew that his sisters, often resentful of his ordering them about, were intrigued by the sudden appearance of a handsome uncle, and too young to care deeply who was head of the family. Pirkka, too, was excited by the adventure and mystery of an uncle he scarcely remembered.

Aslak was exhausted from his trip and saddened by Old Grandmother's death. He longed for a moment to be only a boy and to be comforted. How easy it would be to let his uncle take on all the cares and burdens of the family. For a swift second, he thought if the nuggets matched, he would not dispute his uncle's claim.

But twist and turn the halves as they might, there was no match—even when Uncle Piera impatiently tried to snatch the half from Aslak's hand. Had he managed to get hold of it, Aslak was sure his uncle would substitute the other half of the nugget he had brought—that it was up his sleeve waiting for a split-second sleight-of-hand switch.

Aslak pulled back. "This does not leave my grasp, for I do not trust you to return the right half to me," he said. "It is

clear that we each have half a nugget, but one of them is false. I believe my grandfather never intended to split the herd and leave part to you. But who does have the true half? And where is the other?"

"Tsk, tsk!" muttered the mayor in bewilderment. "The parish laws—"

"—can have nothing to say about nuggets!" declared Aslak. "This is between my uncle and me. But I tell you in all truth that the box of secret belongings of my grandfather, Jouni Magga, is not in this *kåta*. He asked that it be left with him at his burial, but where that place is only my father knew."

A sullen look swept over Piera's face, as he turned to the mayor. "I doubt he tells the truth."

But the mayor knew Aslak and had seen him on his travels

ever since he was a small child. "No—Aslak does not lie."

"My grandfather died on the summer journey," Aslak explained. "My father took his body to the secret resting place of our ancestors, for he had been told how to find it. The knowledge passes from father to son, but when the time came, my father was too ill to tell me. I swear I do not know where it is."

Or had the wizard told him when he said to find the Cave of the Great Hunters in the Mountain of the Eagle's Head?

Then Aslak was silent for a moment. Was Kuisma really a wizard whose trance brought his knowledge? Or was he just a blind peddler, full of intrigue, who had plotted with Piera against Aslak? For according to Piera it was Kuisma who had brought him the half nugget and his father's message.

But if Kuisma and his warning were to be believed, if Piera

had only used Kuisma's name in a lie, then Aslak must be bold and cautious at the same time! So he said, "Since my uncle and I both have half a nugget, let us each mark our own half now and each give his marked half to the mayor, who will keep them both. Then whoever finds the box of secret belongings will take it to the mayor, who will open it and see whose half the nugget in it matches."

When Piera agreed so readily, Aslak wondered if some sleight-of-hand had already taken place. Then he remembered the words of Kuisma, the wizard—and even though he half-doubted and half-believed what he had heard and seen, he knew his only hope was to discover the Cave of the Great Hunters before his Uncle Piera did.

But first they must mourn Old Grandmother and take her body out the rear of the *kåta*, through the opening only used in time of death. For small though a *kåta* was, each place in it had its purpose—the food and utensils and goods always in the same area; the man of the house in one spot by the hearth; the woman by another; children and old people here; friends and strangers there. For no one might enter a Lapp tent without being bidden, nor disturb an empty tent if a log lay across the entrance, showing the owner's absence. Respect for custom was great among his people, and impatient as Aslak was to move his *kåta* and be off on a secret journey, he first took care of his grandmother's rites.

The village was now in a turmoil over the death of Great Jouni's widow, the return of the second son, Piera Magga, and the fate of five orphaned children and the silver reindeer. Aslak could not make open preparations to leave, nor could he whisper his plans to the children, for fear they would innocently give them away.

Anxiously he watched the weather. Moss under the snow was scarce and hard for the deer to find. Each day the forest rang with ax blows as men chopped down pines entangled with the black beard moss of Lapland—so the deer at least could eat that. But still the snow was too deep to take the deer from the forest. Nor did Aslak wish to travel alone on his skis to the mountains, for he distrusted his uncle too much to leave his herd and family behind. They must all go together.

In the meantime, Uncle Piera, saying his return was a shock to his nephew, moved into the teacher's turf-and-timber *kåta*. Every night he sat drinking coffee and telling of his travels to anyone who might come and listen and many did. Even Pirkka, to Aslak's dismay.

On the day when the sun, for the first time since autumn, rose above the horizon, people rushed from their *kåtor* scattered through the forest to the shores of the lake, where they could clearly admire the sun. They laughed and sang. Dogs barked and raced. Boys and girls who attended the teacher's lessons became impatient for school to end. The pastor knew his church would soon be poorly attended and rang his bell for service all the harder.

Aslak felt the sun's brief warmth for four days and on the fifth, after the evening meal, he lingered at the hearth.

"I am going to the teacher's," said Pirkka, "to listen to the tales men tell."

"Go," said Aslak. "But if Terhi comes and stands at the door, step quietly outside at once and obey her message."

When Pirkka had gone, Aslak said to his sisters, "I know you are brave and will do what I say. Tonight we leave for the spring camp, for we must reach the far mountains quickly this year. We will prepare everything now and force the deer off if we must. But I shall leave twenty deer to Uncle Piera, as he is too greedy not to accept them and they will keep him longer on the trail than if he traveled alone. Now I will put six sledges here by the *kåta*. Pack four quietly. In the first Terhi will ride with Petri. The last will carry the tent poles. Pirkka and Small Jouni will drive the herd tonight. Merja and I will lead the string of sledges. When all is ready here, we will fetch Pirkka and depart."

Quickly the girls packed the sledges, or *akjor*, with boxes and cooking pans, food and furs. Aslak quietly rounded up the *härkar*, deer broken to bear burdens and pull sledges. He tied cloth around the clappers of their bells, in order to keep them silent. Now he was glad their *kåta* was farthest away from the church and the log school and the teacher's hut. When one of the dogs yipped, he shushed it.

But the sound that worried him most was that of the deer—the grunts they would make, like thousands of complaining, bronchial old men, and the click-click-click of their hoofs as they ran. As it was not the touch of hoof to ice that made the noise, but the vibrating of a tendon over a bone inside the

hoof, there was no way of disguising it. It was one of the deer's ways, along with a musky odor and a flash-light white tail, of finding each other in storm and mist.

In quick time the household was packed and as Aslak and Merja pulled down the cloth of the *kåta* and loaded the poles on the last *akja*, he sent Terhi to bring Pirkka. That boy loved the bustle of the winter village and the schoolmaster's books. He would be lonely on the trail and lonelier than ever when he heard Aslak's plan. But he came, and seeing the preparations, he followed Aslak's orders.

"Quietly we shall lead this string through the forest and wait on the lake. Find Big Horn, the herd leader, and tie his bell so it will not ring and then Shaggy One, the herd follower. Drive Big Horn toward the lake with your lasso and make sure Shaggy One follows. Then the rest will go, and Small

Jouni will keep them together."

"The dogs will help."

"Not this time!" Aslak showed Pirkka four unhappy dogs, all muzzled. "We cannot risk their barking. Someone might try to stop us from leaving the village, and we must have a full day's start on Piera Magga."

"Aslak, why do you fear him? Don't you think he means what he says? That if he is head of the family, he will provide for us all?"

"I not only distrust him, I am warned against him. You must believe me, Pirkka, and do as I say. And before you and Small Jouni begin to drive the main herd, count off twenty and leave them in the corral for strays beyond the church. Here is a message to hang around the neck of one, saying they are the gift of Aslak Magga, head of the family, to Piera Magga. Then let us hope no one finds them before morning."

Fortunately a wind rose and wailed through the trees, bearing the sounds of the deer away from the teacher's hut, where men now sat, chanting a *joik* about the sun's return.

The touch of sun in the daytime had softened the snow crystals so the cold dark of night brought a crust. With cloven hoofs the deer could run once more across the crusty snow—and the sledges could swing along to their gallop. Aslak and Merja on their skis guided the string of sledges, or *rajd*, while Pirkka and Small Jouni skied close to the herd.

Above the stars gave little light, for they no longer burned with the stirring glitter of the Christmas skies. But the frozen snow cast a glow of its own as they rushed over lakes and bogs, through stands of stunted pines snowed into the shapes of trolls, past bare-branched willows flogged by winter gales, and on and on and on.

At last the far white hilltops caught the sun's first fire. Aslak stopped to unmuzzle the dogs and untie the herd leaders' bells. Then, leaving the string of sledges to Merja, he raced ahead to guide the herd away from the open plain to the shelter of a stunted forest. The day's warmth melted the crust and the deer could no longer quickly cross the snow. They rested and grazed.

But there was no rest for the four big children and Small Jouni. The sledge *härkar* were turned loose to forage; the *kåta* poles were put up and its canvas wrapped around; the fire was made and the cook-kettle hung on its chain. They took turns eating and sleeping and watching the deer.

WHEN ASLAK WAS WITH THE HERD, he spent as much time searching the horizon to see if they were followed as he did looking for strays or attacking lynxes and wolverines. And with the night they packed again and harnessed again and traveled again, northward and westward. They went this time with dogs racing and barking and all the bells ringing, for in the vast loneliness of the Arctic night sounds were brave and comforting things.

To Aslak's joy it snowed for three days, not hard enough to keep them from traveling, but enough to cover their tracks. With each day's journey farther from the winter village, Aslak felt more confident. The exhilaration of the air and the continual movement about him kept him full of excitement and energy.

But soon he was faced with a problem. While Terhi and Small Jouni watched the herd, he sat by the hearth talking to Merja and Pirkka. Beside him, Petri played with a puppy.

"In two days we should come to Great Jouni's camp by the lake. Always before we have stayed there in spring to prepare for the summer trek to the mountains and again in autumn to make the winter preparations."

"It will be good not to travel every day," said Merja.

"But Great Jouni's camp is well-known, and anyone looking for us will go there first," said Aslak. "I don't think we should stay there."

"Who will be looking for us? Just why did we leave in the dark, and why have you rushed us over the *fjells* as if Stalo-the-monster were chasing us? So early in spring there are only stray hunters and trappers about. Why should they bother us?" Pirkka asked.

"It is Uncle Piera who will hunt us down. He did not believe me when I told him I don't know where Great Jouni is buried. So he will follow me, expecting me to lead him to the burial place," Aslak reasoned. "Then if I find it, I don't know what will happen, Merja. He is an evil man. Perhaps he will trick me out of the nugget, should it be there. Perhaps he will simply kill me and take it away."

Merja was suddenly terrified to think of her mysterious uncle as a man who could be so ruthless. "Then why did you make us leave the village, where the mayor and the elders could protect us? Why have you brought us here, for if he kills you, he will probably kill us, too."

"So I can pit whatever strength and cunning I have against him. Out here it is just between him and me. The mayor and the elders at the village were too taken in by his promises. Besides, he could have prevailed on the elders to send you to school."

"I would like that," said Pirkka.

Aslak's eyes dimmed in despair. "Maybe I've done the wrong thing, dragging you with me. But I thought you felt as I do—

that this is our life and no man can take it away from us without a struggle. I swore it to our father at his death—so I must try to keep the Magga family and the deer together. Help me, Pirkka. Help me, Merja. And I swear to you that it will be a better life than watching the world go by from a village window all your years."

But he could see they were doubtful. The hardships of the journey brought them no reward—no mother's comfort, nor father's praise, nor worldly goods.

Then Merja said, "There's no sense in going back. So we can only keep on and see what happens. But let us go to the spring camp, Aslak. We must—the meat we need for our journey is stored for us there."

"With a thousand deer anyone can find us anywhere in Lapland!" Pirkka pointed out. "Uncle Piera showed me his telescope once, and how you see the feathers one by one on an eagle far overhead. He can find you no matter where you hide! So does it matter where we camp?"

"That is probably true," Aslak sighed. The children's doubts and the enormity of his undertaking began to weigh on him.

"And remember," said Merja, "the does will soon have their calves, so we cannot travel every day. We should stay at the camp and rest. The herd has a rhythm of its own and that we cannot change. If you tried and lost the new calves, then the elders would say you were too foolish to be the head of the household."

So they decided to stay the usual time at the camp.

It was by a lake on the south slope of a rolling hill where

patches of pale, spongy moss were already free of the snow. The bucks were separated now from the does, and all the deer rested and gathered strength. The dogs sniffed for old bones. The children, too, looked forward to a feast, hoping no animals had stolen the supply of reindeer meat slaughtered and frozen in the fall and stored in wooden shelters built atop high posts.

But when Merja saw the three storehouses, she cried, "Look! Broken into! The doors are ripped off and half the meat is gone!"

"How high the snow must have been for the wolverines to reach it!" said Terhi.

Aslak said little, but when he had time he brought a ladder and looked closely at the doors. "There are no claw marks on the wood. I do not think it was four-legged animals who took the meat."

Merja, too, as she swept out the *kåta*, made of turf-and-timber, felt someone had used it after they had left in the autumn. It was a dread feeling, making even the familiar dwelling seem strange and uncomfortable. She threw out every old twig, sending Terhi and Petri to the dwarf willows and birches by the lake to gather fresh ones. When Petri brought her a funny stone

with a face he had found on the shore, Merja set it defiantly in the same place where Old Grandmother had kept her good-luck gods.

"Please take away the feeling of the unknown which is in this house," Merja suggested politely.

"Perhaps it was only someone who took refuge in a storm!" said Pirkka, for that was permitted.

"I hope no one comes while we are here now!" Merja said, picking up Petri and hugging him close for comfort.

"I will protect you," said Pirkka. "Anyway, we are safe in this *kåta*." He pointed to the high log doorstep and low log lintel. Anyone entering had to bend his head at the same time he stepped up and over, so a stranger could be clubbed senseless before he had both feet in the door.

But the children felt safe enough so they could fall asleep after a good meal of reindeer meat stewed long and drawn steaming from the cook-kettle.

Each day the sun's goodness pushed back the snows as well as the hours of darkness. Soon the does, the *vajor*, began to drop their young, and the children counted the stick-legged

calves struggling up from the snow. While one child slept, the others watched—to make sure that bears, awakened hungry from their winter sleep, did not eat the calves. Even Petri was put on the back of a *härke,* where he could be safe but see over the herd, and told to cry out if he saw any animal but a deer or a dog.

Aslak, looking out over the *fjells* and the lakes and the bogs, remembered that it was days since he had seen a tall tree, and he was conscious of time, for he wanted to hurry the herd on to the mountains. He wondered in what fold of the *fjells* his Uncle Piera lurked and whether he had in his greed kept the twenty reindeer with him.

Yet so far in all the empty earth about him he could see no other herd, no other people. There was nothing but the sky; and in starlight or sunlight, peacefully moonlit or tumultuous with clouds, it was a tremendous arc above and beyond the limits of the eye at the farthest horizon.

But there was other work to do besides keeping watch. Small Jouni tarred the six sledges again to make them waterproof, and then stored them away. Halters and reins and packsaddles needed repair. Aslak and Pirkka both needed new lassos, cut and braided from good deerskins.

This was the time of the year when their mother and grandmother had made new boots and mittens, woven bootlaces and belts, and twisted root fibers into the patterned mesh of cheese molds. Merja cried when she thought of Old Grandmother sitting by the hearth, pulling out dried deer sinews and twisting and rolling them against her cheek to make thread. For now it was all she could do to mend their boots and mittens, and cook their food and count the calves and milk the does and make cheese for their next journey.

Because the sun barely dipped into enough dusk for them to rest, she worked long hours and her only pleasure was to sit late in the evening by the lake and listen to the thrush and bluethroat sing.

Ice melted, and fish in the nearby streams and the lake made a tempting change from their year-round diet of reindeer meat, which they ate braised and stewed with herbs in the cookpot; or smoked and dried and chewed down cold many a time on their journeys.

One evening Pirkka lay motionless on a rock by the lake and saw a large pike in the shallows. He knew he should run to find a net. Then he felt the sudden chill of a shadow and heard a body brush against the rock.

"The fish is there," he whispered, expecting to see Aslak's

hand cast out a net. Instead a large brown paw thrust out before him and a huge fur shoulder passed close enough to warm his face as a bear plunged upon the fish.

Pirkka shook to think the great beast must have stood behind him as he dreamed. Breathlessly he slid from the rock and stepped silently as a lynx. Outside the *kåta* Petri played with a pile of stones and Pirkka picked him up and plopped him inside.

Merja looked up from braiding a belt, startled.

"What is the matter?"

"A big bear is fishing in the lake. He nearly fished me. Where is the gun?"

Pirkka had shot wolves and wolverines, and he knew it was dangerous for a boy barely five feet tall to shoot a bear almost nine feet tall. The first shot must be the last. He must walk out with the courage of a man.

Pirkka did. He even felt it unfair that the bear should be so busy fishing that he could take him unaware. Then as he approached Pirkka's foot slid on a loose stone, making a sudden *chink* of sound. The bear swung about and saw Pirkka just as the boy took aim. WHAM! Pirkka's shot was true and hit the heart. The bear fell.

Pirkka started toward it, when Aslak, running at the sound of the shot, called out, "Wait! Bears are treacherous. Let me see first if he is really dead."

Aslak fetched a ski from the edge of the snow field and prodded the bear. Then he called in Small Jouni, and together they skinned it, while Merja roasted some meat. Aslak told Pirkka they would cure the skin and he could keep it or sell it at the

winter fair. "With such a brave brother to help me, how can the mayor say we should give up our herd and go to school!" Aslak praised him.

Pirkka was so full of joy in his accomplishment that he sat on the rock in the evening sunlight, making up a *joik* about wonderful Pirkka, the bear hunter.

"You are boasting!" laughed Terhi, who sat with him, holding a sleepy Petri. "Many men shoot bears."

"But this is my first," insisted Pirkka, "and it is big enough for a song."

As the days lengthened, ice and snow sank into the earth and the streams roared and boiled in their stony beds. Suddenly spring buds appeared, and Aslak, watching this time with a man's eyes instead of a child's, understood why his people believed so long in magic. For spring became summer in a single day, as if an incantation changed bud to full leaf while he watched. In hours the wand-bare birches became fully clothed in green, and the willow's leaf burst out as bright as sunlight. The cuckoo called out, "Summer is here."

But with all the glory of the new life shooting up through the *fjells* came the pests—the midges and horseflies, mosquitoes and gadflies—pests of the people and enemies of the deer, for the sting of the gadfly injected eggs under the reindeer's skin that hatched to torment and sometimes kill the deer. And the mosquitoes hummed in swarms, hovering around deer and humans like a horrid outer garment. Awake or asleep, it was impossible to escape them.

The insects were the sign Aslak awaited to tell him it was time to move to the farthest mountains.

"Ahead lies a difficult journey," he told his brothers and sisters. "And we must seek new trails and find a summer camp by ourselves."

"Oh, Aslak! Why can't we stay near our friends as we always do!" Merja begged.

"I know there is a boy from Kaaresuvanto you long to see again," Aslak teased gently. "And if I can find what I seek in time, we will join the others before the summer roundup. But we must go alone and stay alone while I search for the Mountain of the Eagle's Head."

"I have never heard of that," said Merja.

"Nor had I," said Aslak.

"Aslak Magga!" called a voice just outside the *kåta*. "Let me come in."

The children's hearts jumped with fright. But Aslak rose quietly, his hand on the sharp-pointed *puuko* sheathed at his belt. Who stood outside? Who heard him speak of the Mountain of the Eagle's Head? He hoped it was not his uncle.

Even so his heart missed a beat when he saw blind Kuisma with the owl on his shoulder and the dog at his side. But Aslak invited him in. Petri cried at the sight of the owl, and the puppies snarled at the intrusion of the strange dog. The *kåta* was a small dark place to hold such noise and confusion, but at last all settled down. Terhi gave Kuisma a bowl of stew.

Merja, who knew Kuisma only as the blind peddler, cried, "Tell us who you have seen and where you have been! Do you know if our friends from Enontekio and Kaaresuvanto are coming this way?" And both girls begged to see the gay ribbons he brought for sale in his pack.

Aslak let them ask their girlish questions, but when they were through, he told Kuisma to follow him to the lake, and began abruptly, "Since you know all, tell me where is my Uncle Piera and what is he doing?"

"Ah, my boy!" The old man's face was as wrinkled as the lake in the wind. "How can I tell you that? For I am only a blind peddler, carrying my pack from camp to camp. And your uncle has no camp that I have seen."

"You mean he is free of a herd? He can travel swiftly and alone?"

"I am told he kept six of your *härkar* for a sledge string and four bucks for racing and gambling. He sold the rest to buy food and supplies for his search. He left the winter village not long after you, telling the mayor he would meet him at the summer roundup—bringing Great Jouni's box of secret belongings and the other half of the Karasjoki nugget, which he expects to find wherever your granfather is buried."

"Then without a full herd and does and young calves to watch over, he can have searched the whole of Lapland before I can even see the mountains on the horizon!" Aslak hit the rock by which they stood in anger. "And how do I know, since you acted as go-between with my grandfather's message and handed him that half-nugget of gold that you have not also told him of the Cave of the Great Hunters in the Mountain of the Eagle's Head! How do I know that you have told me a true thing?"

"What message? What half-nugget of gold? When was I a go-between for your grandfather? Aslak, you are sorely tried and worried, or you would not speak so," said the old man sadly. "Did I ever tell you that I gave Piera Magga a nugget and a message?"

"No! I did hear it from his lips, not yours! Forgive me, but I have not known whom to believe. Then you have not told my uncle about the Cave of the Great Hunters or the Mountain of the Eagle's Head?"

"I have told him nothing. Nor would he listen to a blind peddler. He has used me in his lies because he is fool enough to think his word worth more than mine. But I know all about him. I know he has hidden around the countryside these seven years, living in the camps of others, stealing reindeer for food. I know much and my drum told me more."

"Then will you use your drum again? If I could only know which pass in the mountains leads to the cave."

"When I crossed the lake to the village to mourn the death of my old friend your grandmother, my drum was stolen. Perhaps by Piera, who has no respect for sacred things and hopes to sell it for gold. And without it I am only poor blind Kuisma, the peddler. You must find my drum for me, Aslak, so I may be Kuisma the wizard once more."

Aslak sighed. How much more would fall upon his shoulders? How much could he accomplish with the burdens he bore of children and a herd of deer and treacherous rivers and mountains to cross? A loon sat upon the lake and shrieked with such laughter that Aslak shivered.

Kuisma spoke. "I tell you to start upon your summer trek at once. You will know the Mountain of the Eagle's Head when you see it. But be careful lest you take an easy way which will prove disastrous. I will wait for you at the summer roundup."

Then the owl took flight from his shoulder, the dog padded ahead, and the peddler followed them over the *fjells*.

NOW THAT THE SNOW HAD MELTED from the *fjells*, more *härkar* were harnessed and burdened, for sledges could no longer be pulled and everything must be borne by the deer. Aslak and Pirkka tied things on carefully, so nothing would slip as they climbed the mountain passes, or be torn off as they swam the savage streams.

Now, with the sun never falling from sight, they could travel at any hour, stopping at any time to pitch their tent, eat and sleep. Small Jouni and the dogs stayed close to the herd, while Aslak often climbed higher places by himself to study the range of mountains on the horizon.

"I wish I had a telescope like Uncle Piera," he sighed. "I wish I had listened more to father when he talked about his journeys. Once we cross the next stream, I must find a new way through the mountains so we will be above and beyond the summer camp grounds."

"But why couldn't we go to camp with our friends? The deer would be safe there, and you could leave us while you searched by yourself?" Merja pleaded. "It would be quicker and easier."

"Quicker and easier, yes," Aslak answered, remembering Kuisma's warning. "But it would not be safe." He did not say it aloud, but if he were by himself his uncle could push him over a cliff or drown him in a torrent and no one would ever know it was not another sad accident to Great Jouni Magga's unfortunate family.

Except for the click of the reindeer's hoofs and the clack of their bells or the shriek of a buzzard whose silent world was startled by the caravan, it was a quiet journey until they came to a mountain brook, or *jokk*. Terhi shivered to hear its threatening shout long before she saw it, for this was where their mother had drowned. In late summer the stream would have barely enough water to wash its stones. But now, swollen with

melted snow fields and cruelly cold, savage with the rush of raging rapids, the water screamed defiance as it hurtled past.

Aslak and Pirkka added to their weight by putting stones inside the spacious pocket made by the top of their belted tunics. Then they helped Small Jouni start the herd across. Even strong Big Horn, the herd leader, had to be shoved and Shaggy One, the herd follower, coaxed to start the procession, for the *jokk* was furious in its force. The weakest calves were swept and tumbled down the stream. When three were crushed and drowned before he could save them, Small Jouni cried.

Back and forth through the icy, waist-deep water went Aslak, shouting and encouraging until all the herd spread out on the other side to graze. Then he and Pirkka tightened the *härkars'* packsaddles once more and with a slap on the rump urged them into the swirling stream.

Terhi was frightened, and Merja tried to calm her. They pulled their skirts as high as they could and squealed as the icy water filled their boots and pushed at their knees. When they were waist deep, they stopped squealing, for the cold clutched away their breath.

Pirkka splashed and scrambled next, and then Aslak, making sure nothing was left behind, swung Petri onto his shoulders, holding him tight by the legs.

"Be careful! You've pushed my hat over my eyes!" he scolded. Petri pulled it back. Step by slippery, shivery step, Aslak crossed the stream and dropped his little brother thankfully on dry ground. Another year, another crossing!

In the warm sun they dried out their soaking tunics and leather pants. They spread out the sedge-grass with which they filled their boots instead of wearing stockings. They put up the dripping *kåta*, splashed by the churning water, cooked a hot meal and slept—all but Aslak, who kept himself awake worrying about crossing the mountains ahead, and Small Jouni, who counted and recounted the herd.

When they set out again, Aslak bravely turned them northward instead of westward. "Once I remember our grandfather telling of a journey made in a spring of such floods that he had to cross all the streams much higher in the mountains and he found a series of passes in mountains which from afar seemed to have no passes at all—just great jagged heights. Beyond was a plateau with a small lake, and he spent most of the summer there before journeying south to the roundup. So we will go north until I see a mountain chain that looks impassable." Again he remembered Kuisma's warning not to take the easy way.

Merja was afraid and shook her head. But she did not argue now with her brother. On the trail there were hard decisions to make, and she saw that Aslak suffered over them even more than they all suffered from the insistent biting of mosquitoes and the long hours of tiresome walking.

On the rolling trackless *fjells,* Aslak could relax and say, "We will follow the deer." He could study the herd, and sometimes carry a weak calf for a way.

But at the edge of swift streams, he must tie a lasso around his waist and, giving Small Jouni the other end with which to pull him in like a wounded fish if necessary, he must test the currents and sudden deep drops until he was sure the children and burdened deer could cross.

For a few days they followed a stream that wandered toward the northwest. One evening Aslak walked ahead, trying to decide where to turn away from its roaring bed. Pebbles and stones were rough beneath his feet, and as he stood there staring down he saw a nugget of gold. He picked it up and a plan suddenly filled his mind. He smashed the nugget in two and placed the pieces in his hat.

In the next days, they turned west and soon were climbing up, until peaks that had been a distant blue rose overhead, black rocks. Usually Aslak loved the mountains, for in them he felt far above the world and free of it. Enchanted by space, he could forget the heavy weight of winter crushing them under its darkened sky. But on this trek he worried lest a rocky ledge stop at the edge of nothing, or stones loosened by wind and weather fall and frighten the deer into a stampede. The winds were high and mournful, and the loneliness was unending.

Yet each time Aslak said, "I cannot see where this day's journey will end," a pass opened out.

But one day he looked ahead in dismay. "There is a glacier!"

he told the others. "A small one. But dangerous. Yet we must cross it. And beyond—that is a snow field full of crevasses. We must camp here and take only a few deer at a time."

Untying the skis from one of the *härkar*, Aslak began the treacherous task of guiding the deer and the children. Each time the passing of the deer made that trail unsafe, he sought a new track before bringing the next deer across. Back and forth he went, until at last they were all safe on the far side. During this, he did not sleep for almost a two-day span. When it was over, he lay down on the first patch of safe ground and slept unmoving in the full blaze of summer night.

Finally they climbed the back of the mountain chain and started down the other side. Below Aslak saw a moorland protected on all sides by mountains. In the middle of the plateau was a lake.

"There!" Aslak exulted. "We have found our camp."

He looked at his weary brothers and sisters. Even Small Jouni was thin and tired, and the deer were more like shadows than beasts. "You are brave! Braver than I had any right to ask. But only one hazard remains—this last steep mountain side."

The deer, free to make their own pace, could breast through the softening snow as through waves. But they could not be allowed to rush on top of each other in panic, for the calves could be trampled and smothered. The *härkar*, too, had to be held back—lest the weight of their packs push them too fast and they lose their footing and roll down the slopes. Going down with sledges would have been even more dangerous, and ropes would have been tied on the runners for brakes. But

Aslak had left the sledges behind, for he had not realized his route would take them through so much snow.

Yet it was the snow fields on the lower slopes which saved the deer from the tortures of insects. Some Lapps nearer the sea always took their herds to islands even though the deer had to swim across deep *fjords* to reach them. But Aslak's people used the mountain snow fields instead, for the deer could climb away from the insects in the day's warmth. These were the snows that never melted even on the warmest longest summer days—the eternal snows. Aslak, whose life was made up of ceaseless change, found the fact this snow was always there, oddly comforting.

Terhi and Petri delighted in their private camp ground, and in the tiny flowers and berries they found all around. But Merja was sad. She looked forward each summer to seeing friends among the Lapps who journeyed from other regions to the same great plateau, now miles away from her.

Pirkka, too, missed the visiting from tent to tent, the summer lessons with the schoolmaster, and the competition to see who could lasso calves the quickest. He hoped they would arrive in time for the great roundup, where all the herds were sorted out in an uproar of excitement—dogs barking, deer grunting, dust rising, men yelling, lassos swishing, and girls cheering!

But Small Jouni was content. He would spend his summer hours sleeping and fishing and carving knife handles and spoons and needle cases from reindeer bone and horn.

They ate salmon and trout from brooks and sour-sweet seedy cloudberries from bogs, and lay back in carpets of heather and mountain forget-me-nots. Pirkka and Terhi brought out the wooden *tablo* board and played a game of "catch the wolf" with reindeer toe bones as the playing pieces.

But Aslak walked to the snow fields, put on his skis, and climbed to a high peak, where he sat staring out over the mountains which seemed to ring the world. There was a crag as sharp as a buzzard's beak, and there a range as solid as a bear's back. But where stood a mountain with the shape of an eagle's head?

As he became more familiar with the mountains, he decided

there were three that might be the right shape, but they were all in different directions. He felt an urgency to start out at once, but he realized it might be a long search, and there were things to take care of first with the herd.

Then one day he saw a light flash up from a mountain nearby again and again. He wondered if it was the sun striking the lens of a telescope and if his uncle had discovered them. That night Petri's puppy in the *kåta* barked until he set the herd dogs barking.

"Is someone lurking around the camp?" Terhi asked.

Merja sighed. "I wish someone were. It is so lonely here by ourselves."

"I'm afraid Piera Magga has found us and is watching everything we do," worried Aslak.

The next morning a good lasso, left by the skis on the snow field, had been taken. Aslak was sure then that his uncle was near, for no one else would steal.

"At least if Piera Magga is watching me, he has not found

Grandfather's burial place yet." Aslak found comfort in that. "But how can I leave the camp and begin my search without his seeing and following me?"

"Are you going to search soon?" asked Merja, anxious that it should be done so they could start their journey southward.

"Just as soon as the new calves are marked," promised Aslak, for important as his mission was, the herd still must come first.

So the next days he spent with Pirkka and Small Jouni up on the snow fields. With a swish of the lasso, Aslak caught a calf by the hind legs. Small Jouni tipped it gently to the ground, careful not to bruise its delicate new horns. Swiftly he cut the nicks of Great Jouni Magga's mark in one ear. Aslak saved a

snippet from each, and when all the calves were marked, he threaded the snippets on a string and counted them.

"Four hundred!" For a moment his tiredness vanished, for reindeer were the true wealth of the Lapp. They were his food, his clothing, his transport, and his trade. Aslak had done well to bring so many new calves safely to a summer pasture over such a long and hazardous route. In his joy he said, "Merja, you shall have ten deer of your own to trade at the winter fair—for any pretties you want. Shawls and ribbons and brooches—"

Lonely as she felt, Merja praised Aslak then for his accomplishments.

"I shall sleep awhile," he told her, "but when I wake I will set off. I may return in a day or a week. But if I do not return in two weeks, then wait no longer. Pack up the camp and drive the herd south. It will be hard traveling, but you should reach the summer camp in time for the roundup. Then hire two herdsmen to help you journey to the winter village. Once you are there do as you think best. Sell the herd and go to school if you like. But I do swear to you that Piera Magga has no right to this herd."

Then Merja became frightened, for she saw how much it meant to Aslak to prove he owned the herd and could provide for his family. And she was frightened by what he meant—that he must go on a dangerous and lonely quest and might not return.

While they talked, a sudden storm swept over them, clouds closing around the constant sun and throwing shadows violently over the mountains. The whole sky thickened and darkened, while lightning burst about them. In the *kåta*, silver spears of rain thrust through the smoke hole, while Petri clutched his puppy and Terhi clutched Petri. But Aslak went about his plans, gathering food for his trip—dried reindeer milk so rich it was always diluted with water; dried meat and smoked fish; cheese kept in leather pouches. He stored it all inside his tunic, where his belt kept it from falling out. In the points of his cap were coffee beans, rock sugar, and the nugget he had found on the river bank and split in two. He sharpened his *puuko* and threw a lasso over his shoulders.

"Pirkka, I leave you the gun. You will need it on the homeward journey against lynx and wolverine."

"God save you!" said Merja.

"Stay in peace," replied Aslak, and stepped out of the *kåta*.

At that moment a flash of lightning traced the tops of the mountains to the east and south. Among the peaks was one of the three he wanted to explore because its shape could be that of an eagle's head. Again the lightning emphasized its form, and he suddenly was convinced that was the place. Perhaps, like his ancestors, he should trust a sign brought by a storm as much as if it were a message brought by a drum.

He called Merja and Pirkka and pointed the mountain peak out to them. "It is nearer than I thought. If I find the cave there, I should return in a week. Merja, you must do all the things I have told you."

But as he looked at her in farewell, he saw how he could perhaps fool his uncle. "Quick! Lend me one of your dresses. Take my other tunic and wear it for two days. You can hide your long hair in my other cap. I will put on your dress and start away as if I were you, going up to milk the deer. If Uncle Piera is hanging about, he will see two boys at work and not realize I have gone away."

Merja enjoyed a part to play and delighted in Aslak's short tunic and breeches. Aslak felt foolish with Merja's skirts over his clothing and her red cap with its ear flaps nodding in the way. But he wore them until he had walked a day's journey and then bundled them also into his tunic.

He stopped at last to rest, and after a few hours' sleep the scream of an eagle woke him. He saw a small brown lemming trying to escape the searching bird.

ASLAK MADE HIS SECOND DAY'S JOURNEY at a steady pace until he reached the snow field below the peak of the mountain which was his goal.

Under a huge rock he left his sister's dress and hat, and much of his food, for he knew a hard climb stretched up above him. He wished for his skis as he sank deeply into the snow without them. He wished, too, for his eyeshades of deerhorn scraped thin to soften the glare of the sunlight on snow. There were crevasses, which he had to leap across or climb around, but at last he reached the rocky mountain top. Where was the Cave of the Great Hunters? And what would he find there?

Above him was rock so steep no snow could cling to it. A wind-whipped ledge lay under his feet, leading up in a spiral path to a shadowy crevice that stared blackly out of the cliff like the eye of an eagle. Aslak climbed wearily to the cleft and walked into an arching cave.

Turning from the dazzle of snow and sun outside, he was suddenly as blind as old Kuisma. But when at last he could see in the dimness, he knew it must be the Cave of the Great Hunters, for painted with a red-brown stain on the stone walls were

primitive drawings of reindeer and men. And against the back of the cave, preserved in the eternal cold which even now needled Aslak's bones, lay the body of his grandfather, and beyond another, and another. Aslak bowed his head in the presence of his ancestors and felt sorrow in his heart that his own father, who knew of this place, was not resting there. For here was the unconquerable pride and wildness and mystery of his race, the Samer, and of his family, the Magga—and Aslak felt that whoever stood humbly there received new courage and strength and faith.

Had his uncle reached the cave before him? Aslak hesitated to disturb his ancestors. But on his grandfather's chest lay a small box. Aslak carried it to the light at the cave mouth and opened it. Inside were good-luck stones and wooden charms strung on deer sinews, and—a half-nugget of gold. He saw also the wide ring of gold which his grandfather had always worn with pride.

Aslak took the ring and half-nugget from the box, wrapped them carefully in moss and a cloth he had brought, and put them in a peak of his hat. Then from his hat he took the larger piece of the nugget he had found and smashed, and placed it in the box. Promising himself that next summer he would return the box to his dead grandfather's clasp, he tucked it now inside his tunic.

Too cold to rest in the cave, he began the downward journey, elated that he had found the sacred resting place and the half-nugget with which to prove himself head of the family.

Forgetting caution, for in all that day's journey the only voice he had heard was the scream of an eagle, he began a *joik* of thankfulness and joy. Even as he plodded through the snow field he hummed a song, and he stopped singing only as he came at last to the rock where he had hidden his sister's dress and hat. Now he was tired and planned to sleep. But when he bent over to look, he found the dress and the hat were gone.

Fear leaped through his body and left his limbs shaken and weak. Then, as he slowly straightened up, he heard the *whoo-whisk* of a lasso.

He jumped aside barely in time to escape being caught around the neck.

"Ho!" shouted his uncle, who stood above on the rock triumphantly twirling the rope.

Aslak remembered that this man was known for two things—his poor skill at gambling and his superb skill at lassoing.

*Whoo-wheesh!* Before he could move again, the leather circle fell around Aslak's shoulders, and he felt the shock as his uncle jerked it, trying to pull it tight about his neck. He intended to strangle him! But luckily Aslak could reach the knife on his belt, and with a swift slash he cut the lasso before Piera could

tighten it enough to finish squeezing off his breath.

Then Piera leaped from the rock and seized Aslak. He knocked the knife from his hand, and it fell out of sight in a patch of moss. They pummeled each other as Aslak fought to keep his uncle from jerking the cut end of the lasso and breaking his neck.

But his uncle was strong and fresh, and Aslak was exhausted from climbing. His hat fell off and he kicked it under the rock. Then his uncle knocked him down and Aslak fell so heavily on his back that his breath left him and he could not move. Seeing a box outlined under Aslak's tunic, Piera ripped open the boy's blouse and seized it.

Gloating, he held it up, while Aslak lay on the ground, weak and dizzy and breathless. Piera put a heavy foot on the boy's chest to keep him down.

"You are not so smart, Aslak. Did you think I would let you escape me? I'll admit you fooled me when you walked off in Merja's dress and left her behind in your clothes. But like all women, when her sister Terhi washed her hair, Merja had to wash hers, too. It looks very foolish when a figure in a belted tunic suddenly takes off a cap and washes long, long hair. And luckily through my glass I saw you struggling up the snow field this morning. A half-day's walk and I found where you had hidden your costume and heard you singing gaily up above me. And now—you did all the hard work for me and I have the box!" He proceeded to open it. "And there is the other half of the luck of the Karasjoki. Now all Great Jouni's wealth is mine."

Aslak took comfort in having changed the nuggets—knowing that his uncle gloated over a nugget which could prove nothing, for the true nugget was half in his own hat and half in the mayor's safekeeping. But since his uncle had already provided the mayor with his own half nugget, he must also be planning a substitute for the nugget now in the box. That being so, his uncle was apparently counting on the box itself, painted with Jouni Magga's name and designs representing the kill of the biggest bear in all Lapland—to convince the mayor that Piera had found it and was handing him the right nugget.

Aslak saw then that his only chance lay in reaching the mayor before Piera could make his claim. Perhaps his grandfather's ring would be his proof that he was the one who reached the burial place. But Aslak began to feel that it was the truth and right of his tale which must finally convince the mayor.

Yet how could he manage to reach the mayor before his uncle? Piera took his foot from Aslak's chest, and the boy tried to move and could not. A horrifying weakness crept through his body. He wondered if he had broken his back and would be unable to move ever again.

Exhaustion seemed to be overcoming him. He must not let it, but he would use it if he could.

"You have won," he whispered to his uncle. "You have the box with its nugget. You can show it to the mayor at the summer roundup. But since the deer are your wealth, you must take them with you. As you cannot herd them alone, you must take Small Jouni and my brothers and sisters to help on the trail. Besides, you made great promises to the mayor about

caring for them. It would look strange if you came to the camp with several thousand deer and none of us. And what do you intend to do about me? Leave me here to die? I am too weak to move, for when you knocked me down you must have broken my back."

But Piera Magga was not troubled by the boy's plight. "So you cannot move? Then I can only say that on my way back from the burial place of my ancestors I saw you lying on the trail, broken from a fall. And I shall say that I heard your last words. For who else will hear them? Because by the time I reach your camp, you will be dead. No one lives long lying in this cold."

Fear showed in Aslak's eyes that he indeed might freeze to death. Or Piera might kill him then and there. But Piera only kicked him, and even though he wore reindeer-skin boots, the blow sent splinters of pain ranging through Aslak's body. But he did not flicker an eyelash or flinch or show that he felt it in any way.

"You see I am paralyzed and beyond help," Aslak told him.

"So why waste your time with me? Show Merja the box and tell her it makes you head of the family and she must obey you on the trip to the summer camp."

His uncle did not answer, but scrambled about, hastily thrusting his telescope and some of Aslak's supply of food into his tunic, until he looked like an odd-shaped being indeed—as odd and cruel as the dim-wit monster Stalo of the Samer legends. The thought of Stalo and his magic, evil though it was, made Aslak realize it would take some magic for him to carry out the rest of his plan—for he knew he must be hurt, although how badly he could not yet tell. As he stared up at Piera, one of the shapes pushed against his tunic looked familiar.

"Now you have the box, give me the magic drum you are carrying, so I can ask the spirits to help me if I must pass from this world," he begged. "After all, I am your flesh and blood and I lie in the shadow of my ancestors' resting place. You owe me at least that comfort."

If only to be gone the sooner, Piera pulled out the magic drum, dropped it onto Aslak's body, and departed.

ASLAK DID NOT STIR until his uncle had been out of sight a long time. Then as his strength returned, he found he could move. Painfully he crawled to the mossy patch, found his knife and cut the lasso from his neck. Standing, he discovered none of his bones broken, but he was bruised from the fight and aching from his climb. He knew that sleep was the only healer close at hand, so he wrapped himself in Merja's dress, which his uncle had left behind, put his own valuable hat on his head, rolled under the shelter of the rock, and slept.

He awoke to the same bright light of the unsetting sun. Eating dried reindeer tongue and cheese and some rock sugar restored his strength. He packed his few bundles and Merja's clothes inside his tunic. Before he added the magic drum he studied it carefully. It did look like blind Kuisma's, and it would be like Piera to have stolen such a thing from a defenseless man. Aslak tapped his fingers on it softly, and then fearing what he did not know about it, stored it away in his blouse. He set out for the south by a different pass than that his uncle would use for the herd.

He climbed and descended stony ridges and crossed moss-covered plateaus; he found tiny freshets of purest water to drink and occasional berries to eat; he slept when he could no longer march on, and marched on when he could no longer sleep. Part of him found great joy in the freedom of traveling without the chores and worries of the herd and his brothers and sisters. The grandeur of the sky and the mountains gave him peace. But the other part of him worried about his family and the treatment they would receive on the trail from his uncle. He wondered if they would think he really was dead, and how much they would miss him!

After a few days of walking he came to the region where mountains alternated with valleys slanting to the southeast, and the freshets became brooks that sparkled into streams that swept into rivers or swelled into lakes. Soon there should be a river that would lead him to the plateau of the summer roundup. But even if he stood on tiptoe on a peak of the highest mountain, he could not peer beyond the horizon to see which was the right river. The sun rolling about the horizon gave him no clue. There was no one to consult. Aslak had never felt so alone in his life.

But on the next day he saw over the horizon on the southeast a flock of eagles and, deciding to take them as a sign, followed the first brook leading in their direction.

For three days he descended from the mountains, while the voice of the brook changed from its first small babble over pebbles to a deeper conversation with its stones and fish. Now dwarf willows and birches occasionally edged its banks, and with each hour Aslak longed to catch sight of a column of smoke in the sky; or to look up at the white of the snow fields on the lower mountains to see reindeer moving; or to hear a dog bark—for some Lapps measure distance by sound and say that something is as far away as a *baenagulam*, or as far as a dog's bark is heard.

And with each hour he worried more that he had taken a river valley that would not open into the big plateau but cross above it and lead him only to more mountains. He saw no signs that a herd of reindeer had traveled before him, nor heard any sign that they might be close behind. He began cursing himself for entrusting the children and the herd to his uncle's greed. He woke from an ugly dream, thinking that he heard voices, and saw a mother bear fishing in the stream with her cubs. As he was defenseless except for a knife and his lasso, he lay still and did not move until they splashed out of sight.

Then with another day's travel he saw—looking as tiny as the gadflies they sought to escape—reindeer on a snow field far ahead to his left. He shouted for joy and then began a *joik* about

his journey, singing as he ran. And in that burst of happiness, jogging on the bank of the stream, he suddenly slipped on a sharp stone. He heard the crack of a bone as his ankle twisted and he fell heavily. When he tried to stand, he nearly fainted from the pain.

Despair overcame him, for how could he go on? He had no reindeer to ride; no ski-sticks for a splint. He was helpless, while the pain of his leg pushed along his back and weakened his arms. Slowly he dragged himself to a large rock and leaned against it, half-hidden from the passing stream. He fell into dazed sleep.

When he woke he found a mist sweeping down the valley so dense that he could scarcely see across the river. The cold numbed his pain, but he knew it could also kill him. Somehow he had to find help.

Then out of the mist sounds swelled against his ears and

drummed against his mind. The sounds were the clicking of thousands of reindeer hoofs, and the grunting of a large herd. Bells rang through his aching head and dogs barked.

Any second he expected to be engulfed in the rush of reindeer as they dashed past his rock. Surely he could make himself heard to any man who followed them—even if it could only be his uncle. He cried out, "I am here—here! Come and help me!"

Then to his despair he realized the herd was on the farther bank of the river, and the noise was such that no one paid him heed. Nor did anyone see him through the mist.

Aslak knew it could be only one herd—that now led by his uncle. If only he could hear his sisters' voices, high and light as the bluethroat's song, and know they were safely back to the world of people!

But he still must get safely back too. For unless he could be there to tell the truth about all that had happened, his uncle would deceitfully produce the box in which he would have already substituted half a nugget that would match the one marked with his name and now in the mayor's safekeeping. Aslak must find a way to be there!

He wondered if some *kåtor* of the summer camp ground were as near as the sound of a dog's bark. He threw back his head and howled—but there was no reply. The sounds of the herd had long since faded away.

For some time the mist trapped him in desolation, and then silently it disappeared. Shapes of rocks and tiny trees and ptarmigan berry bushes returned. He shifted against the rock, and inside his tunic the magic drum slipped. His elbow struck

it and made it vibrate.

Quickly Aslak pulled it out. Closing his eyes and thinking only of being heard, Aslak beat upon the skin over and over, on and on, until his hand and his arm ached.

When he thought he could go on no longer, there was a rustle of sound, and a white owl floated up from a bend in the river. Then the pad of paws suddenly seemed loud on the stones, as a white dog came to him and threw back his head and howled. And walking over the stones as easily as if they were a solid crust of snow came Kuisma.

"You have found my drum!" Kuisma stopped by the dog and stretched out his hands. Aslak reached up and put the drum into them. "I could feel its beat in my heart and its pulse in my head even as I sat by your mayor's hearth."

"And did you pass my herd and my family, led by my evil uncle, on your way?"

"They are still on the far side of the river from the camp. If you hurry, you can reach the mayor's *kåta* before they swim across."

"My ankle is broken, or I would not have sat here trying to make myself heard with your drum. How am I to hurry when I cannot walk at all?"

"But I have brought a *bärke* to carry you, for I felt your need."

Looking up, Aslak saw a large reindeer waiting in a patch of moss. With Kuisma's help he managed to sit in the saddle, and, holding the pommel tight, he endured the ride to the mayor's *kåta*. Kind hands lifted him down and put him on a bench of twigs and skins outside the door, and fetched him water to drink. But Aslak refused to lie down or take his hat from his head.

"Tell us what has befallen you," said the mayor.

But before Aslak could begin his tale, there was a great commotion at the far river bank. The famous herd of silver deer swam out into the stream, their magnificent antlers like a forest moving over the water. Crossing in a boat were Aslak's two uncles and his brothers and sisters. Straight to the mayor came Piera Magga, the others following him.

When Merja and Terhi suddenly looked up and saw Aslak, they screamed in fright! But Pirkka came running to touch his brother's hand and feel its warmth. He turned to Piera Magga in fury. "How could you tell us such a lie—that you heard our brother's last words—and make us think he was dead!"

Piera Magga stared down at the boys. "So Aslak played a trick on me. He lay there and claimed he was dying. And all the time he intended to let me do the work of bringing down the herd while he ran here by himself. But for what purpose? No matter what lies and tales he has told you since he came, I bring what we agreed upon—the other half of Great Jouni's Karasjoki nugget. It is safely here in his box of secret belongings."

"Aslak has told us nothing," said the mayor. From his tunic he took out a leather pouch and unwrapped two half nuggets—one nicked with the initials of Piera; the other with the initials of Aslak. Kuisma held out his magic drum, and the mayor placed the two halves upon it.

Everyone gathered close as Piera Magga handed the mayor Great Jouni Magga's box. The mayor opened it and took out the half nugget which lay within. "This," he announced, "I take from Great Jouni Magga's box of secret belongings. It is known as the Luck of the Karasjoki and it should fit with the half nugget given me last spring by Piera Magga and marked then as his own."

He picked up the piece marked Piera and after studying it a moment, deftly fitted the halves together.

Terhi and Merja and Pirkka sucked in their breath and waited in suspense to see what their brother would do.

"Of course the two halves would fit!" Aslak spoke quickly. "Because on his travels here with the box he substituted half a nugget that he knew matched the half he had already given the mayor, pretending it was a talisman from his father. A false talisman, for ask blind Kuisma here if his tale of receiving it with a message from his father was not a lie!"

The mayor turned to the peddler. "Is there truth in his tale that you brought him a talisman and a message from his father?"

"None," said the old man.

Aslak cried out, "Seize Piera and search him. For somewhere on his body or in his baggage you will find a half nugget that I can match. For you see I met his deceit with trickery of my own. And it was I who first reached the Cave of the Great Hunters and took the box of secret belongings from my grandfather's clasp. And before I left that cave, I took the true half nugget from the box and placed in it a false one to deceive my uncle."

"You dare not search me!" cried Piera. "You have no right because of a young boy's lie."

"You lied when you told us Aslak was dead!" Pirkka shouted. "You are the one who cannot be trusted."

Two men seized Piera's arms, and Merja said, "Look in the pocket of his *atsaslieppa*, for I saw him take out a nugget and look at it and put it back there only last night when he thought

we were all asleep."

They looked and they found it, and turned to Aslak, who took off his hat. From it he took a small bundle and unwrapped half a nugget. "This will fit the unmatched half now lying on the drum—the half my uncle took from the box when he stole it from me. But it is lucky for me that he was too greedy to throw that half away—for it proves that he stole the box and changed the nuggets."

Piera Magga tried to pull away from his captors. "Do not believe him. He admits to trickery himself. He is only bragging that he reached the burial place of his grandfather."

Silently Aslak took out another little packet from a peak of his hat. Silently he unwrapped the cloth and from the moss inside plucked the ring from his grandfather's hand and the half nugget he had first seen in the cold light of the cave. He handed it to the mayor.

The mayor took up the nugget with Aslak's mark, which he had kept. The halves did fit, just as Aslak said they would.

Merja and Terhi and Pirkka stared at their brother with awe.

"You have won the right to be head of your household and true owner of the silver reindeer," said the mayor. "I believe that you have the right half of the right nugget. But most of all, you proved you have the right in the way you took your deer and your household from our winter village to your summer pasture safely and with an increase in your herd. From now on you will need to make no secret journeys, and the name Aslak Magga will be remembered among men."

PRONUNCIATION

Aslak—Ahs-lak
Jouni—You-ah-knee
Tuure—Doo-reh
Merja—Mare-yah
Terhi—Dare-hee
Kuisma—Kwees-sma
Pirkka, Petri, Piera—all pronounced with the P sounding more like a B, and a nice roll to the R

VOCABULARY

*kata* (sing.) *kator* (pl.) the tent, or hut, of a Lapp
*joik* (pronounced yoi-k) improvised verses for a primitive sort of song
*akja* (sing.) *akjor* (pl.) sledge pulled by reindeer
*härke* (sing.) *härkar* (pl.) the male deer, or ox, who is broken and trained to pull sledges and carry packs
*rajd* (pronounced rahd) a group, or string, of sledges tied together
*vaja* (sing.) *vajor* (pl.) the female deer
*fjells*—the rolling open country
*puuko*—knife with a bone or horn handle
*jokk* (Swedish) or *joki* (Finnish)—river
*baenagulam*—a measure of distance—"as far as a dog's bark is heard"
*atsaslieppa*—an ornamental dickey which fits under the open neck of the tunic. On the inside there is often a pocket for carrying valuables.

LEE KINGMAN is a graduate of Smith College, a former children's book editor, and, in private life, the wife of Robert Natti and the mother of two children. Gloucester, Massachusetts, where she lives, has provided the background for a number of her books. THE SECRET JOURNEY OF THE SILVER REINDEER is the result of a trip Lee Kingman and her family had two summers ago to Finland and Lapland, "a country of mystery," and their rapport with its sturdy people.

LYND WARD is known principally for his woodcuts, although he makes use of many mediums in both adult and children's book illustrations. He was born in Chicago and lives with his author-wife, May McNeer, in Cresskill, New Jersey. But a particular environment which has influenced his work to a great extent is the summer home in Canada, far back in the woods, where he spends the summer every year.